D1426061

Dark Water

Cindy Jefferies

HIGHLIFE HIGHLAND		
3800 11 0085712 1		
Askews & Holts	Feb-2012	
JF	WITHDRAWN	£5.99

A & C Black • London

First published 2012 by A & C Black,
an imprint of Bloomsbury Publishing Plc
50 Bedford Square, London WC1B 3DP

www.acblack.com

Copyright © 2012 Cindy Jefferies
Illustrations copyright © 2012 Dave Shephard

The rights of Cindy Jefferies and Dave Shephard to be identified
as the author and illustrator of this work have been asserted by them
in accordance with the Copyrights, Designs and Patents Act 1988.

ISBN 978-1-4081-5651-3

A CIP catalogue for this book is available from the British Library.

All rights reserved. No part of this publication may be
reproduced in any form or by any means – graphic, electronic or
mechanical, including photocopying, recording, taping or information storage
and retrieval systems – without the prior permission
in writing of the publishers.

This book is produced using paper that is made from wood
grown in managed, sustainable forests. It is natural, renewable
and recyclable. The logging and manufacturing processes conform
to the environmental regulations of the country of origin.

Printed by CPI Group (UK), Croydon, CR0 4YY

recommended by

www.catchup.org

Catch Up is a not-for-profit charity
which aims to address the problem of
underachievement that has its roots in
literacy and numeracy difficulties.

DARK WATER

Contents

Chapter 1

Competition

Sarah filled her lungs with air and dived down. The music was pounding out their sound track as she swam into place. Abbey was turning on the surface of the water, with one leg held high in the air.

Slowly Abbey sank down, hardly making a ripple in the water. For a few seconds the water was still. It was as if the two swimmers had never been there.

Then, suddenly, Abbey shot out of the water, boosted by Sarah below. Abbey held her arms up high. She had a huge smile on her face and it looked as if she was going to leap right out of the pool. As their routine came to a perfect end, and the audience clapped, the girls swam quickly to the side, and got out.

They walked to where their trainer, Mrs Collins, was waiting. She handed each girl a towel. Both girls were out of breath.

The synchronised swimming routine had been very hard work, but they felt happy.

"Well done!" said Mrs Collins. "That last lift was excellent. You are such a good team. I am sure you stand a chance to win a medal."

Sarah and Abbey looked at each other and grinned. If they did well in this competition, they could be picked to train for the Olympics! It was all the two girls had wanted since they had started doing synchro together a few years ago. They hadn't known each other before that. They went to different schools, but Mrs Collins had taught them both synchro since they were little, and had put them in touch with each other.

Two more pairs still had to do their routines. Sarah and Abbey watched closely as their rivals performed. But the other girls hadn't been swimming together as long as Sarah and Abbey, and it showed.

"It's the two girls in the green swimsuits we need to beat," said Abbey as the last pair got out of the pool. "Them and the sisters from York – Sally and Jane Moore. They were really good."

Sarah nodded. "Yes, although neither of them looked as relaxed as we did."

"How can you tell?" teased Abbey. "I might have been frowning during that last lift."

Sarah laughed. "If you were frowning, Mrs Collins would have told you off!"

"That's true." Both girls giggled.

Then everyone went silent as the judges began to announce the results. Suddenly, Sarah didn't feel like laughing any more. If they weren't in the top three they'd feel awful. They'd worked so hard for this, and Sarah wasn't sure they had it in them to improve much more.

Abbey grabbed Sarah's arm, and Mrs Collins put her hands on the girls' shoulders to calm them as they waited. Then the judge announced the top three places.

"Third place goes to Kirsty Emerson and Beverly Hicks."

Abbey squeezed Sarah's arm. "Maybe we've got second."

"Second place goes to Sally and Jenny Moore," said the judge.

Sarah let out a groan. She tried to think if there had been any other pairs who might have been good enough to take first prize. There was a pair from Preston who had been pretty good too.

"And first place goes to… Sarah Plant and Abbey Kirk."

Abbey let out a huge squeal and hugged Sarah. Sarah hugged her back. She couldn't believe it. First place! They'd hoped to come third, or possibly second, but first? That was fantastic!

Chapter 2

If Only

After Sarah and Abbey had got changed,
they hurried to meet Mrs Collins, who was
waiting at the exit.

"Well done," she said again. "First place
is a *fantastic* result. You have a real chance

now of going forward to the Olympics, so we will need to have a meeting to discuss it."

"There's a special training camp, isn't there?" said Abbey.

Mrs Collins nodded. "Yes. If you get picked to join the Olympic swimming team you'll get extra help with training. And you'll get money from sponsors to help cover the costs."

Sarah felt thrilled. None of her family had ever been sporty, or well off. If she had sponsors, it would be a big help. But they weren't quite there yet.

"We need to do really well at the next event, don't we?" she said.

"Yes," said Mrs Collins. "But don't worry. There's plenty of time to prepare."

"I must go," said Abbey. "My parents are waiting."

"Me too," said Sarah, although no one was waiting for her. Her dad worked shifts, her brother never came to watch her, and her mum was at home with the twins, who were too little to come to swimming events in the evening.

"Do you want a lift home?" said Mrs Collins.

Sarah shook her head. "No thanks," she said. "It's not far." She didn't mind the walk. It would give her a chance to think about the

Olympic training camp. Once she got home it would be too noisy to think about anything, with the twins having their bath and her brother's loud music.

On her way home, Sarah saw a boy from her school on the other side of the street. He was a bit ahead of her, and he didn't notice Sarah. But she knew who he was, even from behind. His name was Tom, and he was in her year.

She'd always liked him, even when they were in Year 7. Some of the kids were unkind, and teased people like Sarah, who was shy, but Tom never did. He didn't speak much to her, but Sarah had never minded that.

Sometimes she thought about what it would be like if she and Tom did talk. As she walked along she wondered what he'd say if she told him about her success in the competition. She hadn't told anyone in her class about her swimming, not even the girls. She hadn't wanted anyone to think she was showing off.

Sarah wondered if Tom would go into one of the shops. If he did, she would go in too. They might meet at the check-out and she could at least say hello.

But Tom didn't stop. He crossed the road and went into his house. Sarah went on home, wishing she wasn't so shy.

Chapter 3

Keeping Quiet

The next day, Sarah got to the classroom door at the very same moment as Tom. Before she had time to think about it she smiled at him, and Tom smiled back.

"Another day in the mad house," he said.

The classroom was almost full of students, and very noisy.

"Yes," said Sarah. "And we have to hand in our maths homework."

"Did you finish it?" said Tom. "I thought it was really hard."

"Me too," said Sarah. "And I didn't have much time to do it by the time I'd been to the gym."

Tom looked at her in surprise. "I didn't know you went to the gym." He sounded like he was impressed.

Sarah felt happy. She was talking to Tom! And he wanted to hear what she had to say. They went into the classroom together.

She was just about to explain why she spent time at the gym when there was a burst of loud laughter from a group of boys and girls.

Holly was making a silly face and waving her arms around. "And they all dance around in a circle and wave their arms. That's not a sport!"

Everyone laughed again. Holly looked up and saw Tom and Sarah. "We've just decided that darts and synchronised swimming shouldn't be called sports," she said.

"Fair enough," said Tom. "I've never seen a darts player in a track suit."

"And synchronised swimming is just dancing in the water," said another boy.

"It's not *that* easy," said Sarah.

"That's true," said Holly. "It must take ages to get those silly swimming caps on!"

They all laughed again, including Tom. Sarah felt herself blush, and looked away. She had been about to tell Tom that she was a synchronised swimmer! She wanted to explain to the class that her sort of swimming was very difficult. She had to train for hours every week, not just in the pool, but at the gym too. It was a very tough sport, but she was afraid if she told the students that, they'd still laugh.

Chapter 4

Telling the Truth

After school, Sarah headed to the gym as usual. Every morning she and Abbey trained together in the pool but after school they each went to their local gyms to work on power and strength training.

It was hard, especially when she wore weights on her arms and legs while doing the exercises. But Sarah enjoyed it. She found that all her worries simply faded away while she worked out. She just thought about being as good as she possibly could.

But at the end of her training, when she took the weights off and picked up her towel, she noticed a tall, slim boy, waiting at the desk. It was Tom! He looked as surprised to see her as she had been to see him.

"What are you doing here?" she asked. She hoped he wouldn't notice her sweaty clothes and pink face.

Tom went red. "I thought I'd join the gym.

I didn't think that anyone in our class belonged until you told me this morning. Do you come every week?"

Sarah thought quickly. If Tom joined he'd soon hear all about her. The man who managed the gym kept a record of her results on the notice board. He had even held a raffle to help raise money for her. There was no way she could pretend to Tom that she only came here once a week.

She took a deep breath. She had to tell him the truth, and if that meant that he didn't like her any more, well, that was just too bad.

"I come here six days a week," she told him. "I'm in training. I'm trying to get a place on the Olympic swimming team."

Tom's mouth opened. "Really? I didn't know that. What sort of swimming do you do?"

Sarah pointed to the notice board behind him. There was a photo of her and Abbey standing by the pool in their swimming costumes. The gym manager had just put up the details of their most recent win. Tom went over to the board and studied it. After a few moments he turned round and grinned at her.

"That's fantastic, Sarah! Congratulations. You must have to train ever so hard if you come to the gym every afternoon."

"And I train in the pool every morning," she said.

Tom shook his head. "I thought I'd just come once or twice a week to build up my muscles a bit. You put me to shame!"

"But synchronised swimming," said Sarah. "You think it's silly. Everyone in class was laughing about it, including you."

"I didn't know what it involves," he said. "But it's different now you've explained about the training. I'm not laughing now, am I?"

Sarah looked at him. He wasn't laughing, but he was smiling at her, and her heart did a flip.

"No," she said with a smile. "You're not laughing now."

Chapter 5

Let Down

The next few days were wonderful. Tom and Sarah spent as much time as possible together, although that wasn't easy with all the training Sarah had to do. Mostly, they hung out at school.

Soon everyone in the class had noticed that Sarah and Tom were good friends. He wanted her to tell them about her secret, but Sarah wasn't sure.

"If we get picked for the Olympics, then it'll be different," she said. "I won't mind them knowing then."

"You'll be famous," said Tom. "In the local paper anyway."

"Maybe," said Sarah. The idea was thrilling. "I just hope we make it through the next competition all right."

"I'm sure you will," said Tom. "Can I come and watch?"

"Of course!" said Sarah, feeling happy.

It was wonderful knowing that Tom would be watching.

Then Holly and Jaz walked past. "Hi, you two!" said Jaz.

"Oh, don't encourage them," said Holly. "Tom's no fun any more now Sarah's got her hands on him."

Tom laughed. "Jealousy will get you nowhere," he said to Holly and he put his arm around Sarah's shoulders. Sarah felt as if she'd died and gone to heaven.

But the very next morning something awful happened. Sarah had had a good training session at the pool, and her hair was still damp when she got to the classroom.

Tom wasn't there yet, but she knew he'd be there soon, and she went in with a smile on her face.

"Here she is!" said Holly, with a grin. At first Sarah thought that Holly was trying to be more friendly, but then, Holly started pretending to be a synchronised swimmer, and making a silly face.

"Oh, I'm so clever!" she giggled. "I can go round and round in the water with one leg in the air. Look at me!"

"Careful," said Matt. "Don't forget that Sarah works out at the gym. She's got bigger muscles than me. She might punch you." He flexed his biceps. All the class laughed.

Sarah was very upset. There was only one person who could have told them. It must have been Tom.

"Look at her," laughed Holly. "She's going to cry now she's been found out. What a loser! Fancy thinking she could get into the Olympics!"

Sarah blinked hard, to stop her tears, but Holly gave her no chance to reply. "Wimps like you don't get into the Olympics," she said. "Even as a synchronised swimmer. So don't think you can, you weirdo."

Chapter 6

Difficult Times

"How could you tell them about me?" said Sarah to Tom later. "I told you they'd all laugh. You've given Holly the perfect way to tease me."

"I didn't tell Holly," said Tom.

"Well, you must have told *someone*," said Sarah. "Because I haven't."

Tom sighed. "I did tell Akram," he said. "But he's my mate. He swore he wouldn't tell anyone else. I thought I could trust him, but he must have let it slip to someone, and then it leaked out. I'm sorry."

Sarah was really angry. "How dare you! I told you to keep it quiet. Now I've got Holly teasing me, and her mates laughing at me. And it's all your fault."

Now Tom looked cross too. "Isn't it about time you stood up for yourself?" he said. "They wouldn't laugh if you explained how hard your training is."

"Oh, wouldn't they?" Sarah spat back.
"Why don't you explain, if you're so clever?"
She flung the door open and almost walked
straight into Holly and her friends.

"Ooh! Here she is," said Holly nastily.
"Our very own Olympic star. Where are you
swimming off to in such a hurry?"

"Leave her alone," said Tom.

Holly laughed. "Now she can't even
speak for herself," she told her friends. "What
a total loser."

Sarah didn't wait to hear any more. She
rushed off to the cloakroom and sat on the
bench.

Everything had gone wrong.

Holly was making her life a misery, and now she'd fallen out with Tom. No one understood.

For the rest of that day, Holly carried on teasing Sarah. "I bet you wish you could wear your swimming cap all the time," she said while they were waiting to go into the science lab.

"Why?" asked Sarah.

"Because your hair is so horrible it would be a relief to keep it covered up," said Holly.

Later on that day, a girl called Lucy who was in Sarah's class came up to her and asked, "Do you do synchronised swimming in a team?"

Sarah wasn't sure what to say. Did Lucy really want to know or did she just want to tease her more? Sarah decided to tell Lucy the truth. "I don't swim in a team," she said, "just with one partner."

But before Lucy could say any more, Holly butted in.

"I don't suppose a group would have her," she said. "She thinks she's so good but she's probably rubbish."

Sarah looked across to where Tom was talking to Akram. Either he hadn't heard what Holly had said, or he didn't care about sticking up for her any more.

* * *

Sarah kept seeing Tom at the gym and she wished they could still be friends. Then, one day she had to wait for one of the gym machines because Tom was still using it. She wasn't supposed to rest much during her training and he was spoiling her session.

"Sorry," he said, moving out of her way. He stayed to watch as she put the weights on her arms.

"You're strong enough to stand up to Holly and the others," he said.

"What do you care?" said Sarah crossly.

Tom lost his temper. "Of course I care!" he said. "But I can't do it for you. You have to stand up for yourself. Holly is just jealous of you, that's all."

"No she's not. She thinks what I do is stupid."

"She only says that because she hasn't a hope of being in the Olympics herself," said Tom. "She wishes she was talented like you, Sarah. Can't you see that?"

"Really?" said Sarah.

"Yes," said Tom. He looked sad. "I'm sorry I let you in for this, but I only told Akram because I wanted to boast about you. What you've done is so brilliant." He reached out and she let him take her hand. "I'm really proud of you, Sarah. Can I come to the pool one morning to see you train?"

Chapter 7

Standing Up

Now that Sarah knew that Tom cared
for her she felt brave enough to answer
Holly back. So the next time Holly said that
synchronised swimming was easy, Sarah said,
"You have no idea what you're talking about.

Have *you* ever competed in a swimming event? Have you ever been in a team for *anything*?"

That made Holly look stupid, and she soon stopped making fun of synchronised swimming, especially when Tom backed Sarah up. Instead Holly began to make fun of Sarah and Tom's friendship. Sarah didn't like that very much either, but it wasn't so bad when there were two of them being picked on.

"Don't worry about it," said Tom. "She's only jealous that we're friends." Tom did seem to be able to shrug off anything Holly said, and Sarah tried to copy him.

* * *

"It's almost the end of term," said Akram one very hot day. "We should have a party or something."

"We could have a picnic," said Holly.

"Good idea!" said Tom.

"I'll make a cake," said Lucy. "I'm good at that."

"And I'll bring crisps," said Akram. "I'm good at that." Everyone laughed.

Sarah smiled at Tom. The sun was shining, it was nearly the end of term, and Holly seemed to have forgotten to be horrible for the moment. Life was good.

"Where shall we have the picnic?" said Tom.

"Here!" said Holly. "We can still get on the school field, even when the school is locked up."

"Wouldn't it be more fun to go somewhere that's not school?" said Tom.

"We could go to the park," said Sarah. "It's lovely by the lake this time of the year."

Holly was cross. "I think my idea is best," she said, but the others liked Sarah's idea about the park more.

Sarah wondered if Holly was going to make a fuss, but the others changed the subject and soon they were chatting about picnic food. Sarah grinned at Tom. This was going to be fun.

Chapter 8

Picnic Time

On the day of the picnic the sun was shining brightly. Sarah got home from her morning training and put together the food that she and Tom had decided to take. Soon the doorbell rang, and he was there, ready to go.

"I'll carry the basket," he said, taking it from her. "Here, you take the Frisbee."

"It was a good idea to think of bringing something to do," said Sarah.

"Akram is bringing a football," said Tom.

"And I've got a rug," said Sarah, slinging it over her shoulder. "After my workout I fancy relaxing in the sunshine."

It didn't take long to get to the park. They walked past the playground where small children were having fun on the swings and slides. They came to a large area of flat grass, and beyond that they could see the big lake. Akram was already there with a couple of the other boys, kicking the ball to each other.

"Let's spread the rug out near the lake," said Sarah. "Then we'll be out of the way of the football."

"Good idea," said Tom.

They put the rug down, and soon other people had added their rugs so that there was a large area to sit on. When everyone had arrived they unpacked the food. There were loads of things to eat, but everyone was hungry, and soon most of it was gone.

Tom lay back on the rug and rubbed his stomach. "I am *so* full."

"Here," said Matt, passing him a bottle. "I'm sure you've got a bit of room for a drink."

"Well, maybe a sip," said Tom. "To help all the food down." He sat up again and took the bottle. "Oh!" he cried.

"What is it?" said Sarah.

Tom made a face. "It's vodka or something…in a cola bottle. Hey, Matt, I thought you were giving me cola!"

Matt laughed. "Well, we're not supposed to drink in the park, so I thought I'd put it in this bottle."

Tom handed him the bottle back. "I'll stick to lemonade, thanks."

"How about you, Sarah?" said Matt. "Fancy a drink?"

Sarah shook her head. "No thanks."

"Sarah doesn't drink," said Tom. "Because of her training. It's better for her not to."

"I'll have some," said Holly, grabbing the bottle out of Matt's hand. "You should get a life, Sarah. You're such a goody goody. It makes me sick."

She took a big gulp. Then she took another gulp and laughed in Sarah's face.

Chapter 9

A Very Bad Idea

The sun was hot, and Sarah was feeling sleepy. She lay back on the rug. Most people, including Tom went over to the open, grassy area. Sarah could hear that teams were being picked for football. It sounded fun, but Sarah was too sleepy to join in.

Holly, Matt and a couple of others were drinking on a rug nearby. They had some cans of beer, and the cola bottle was still being passed around.

Sarah wondered if the park attendant would notice what was going on. He probably wouldn't come over to that corner of the park, but he might. She hoped they wouldn't get into trouble. It would be a shame if the afternoon were spoiled.

Sarah let her eyes close. She was falling asleep. Every now and then she could hear Tom's voice, and that made her smile.

Sarah didn't know how long she had been asleep when a loud yell woke her.

"No! Get off me!"

It was Tom's voice, and Sarah sat up quickly to see what was wrong. She saw Matt and a couple of other boys carrying Tom over the grass. At first Sarah thought they were just mucking around but then she realised that Holly was shouting at the boys, telling them what to do.

"Throw him in the lake," she said, laughing loudly. "Then we can watch his girlfriend rescue him."

Akram was trying to stop them. He ran in front and caught hold of Matt's arm. "Don't be stupid," he said. "The lake might not be safe. There's a notice that says no swimming."

Holly laughed at Akram. "Tom can swim, can't he?" she said. Then she looked at Sarah. "And even if he couldn't swim, Sarah would dive in and rescue him. Look at her. She's already thinking of showing off and jumping in."

Chapter 10

Trapped

Sarah stood up. She didn't know what to do. She didn't want to embarrass Tom. She was sure he wouldn't want her to interfere. But it looked as if nothing was going to stop the boys from throwing him in the lake.

Akram had given up, and was watching from the edge of the lake.

Sarah knew that Tom was a good swimmer. So if the boys just dropped him, it would all be over in a few minutes. She watched as they pulled him further out. Soon they had to let him stand up, because the water was too deep to carry him. But they still didn't let go. They seemed to have forgotten about throwing him in. It had become a splashing play-fight, with even Tom starting to laugh as they all got wetter and wetter.

Sarah relaxed. She guessed that as soon as they were all tired of the play-fight they'd come out and lie on the grass to get dry.

At least the sun was hot enough to dry their clothes.

Tom had got an arm free, and was splashing Matt, who turned round and splashed Tom back. They both laughed. Then, suddenly, Matt vanished. One moment he was there, and the next moment he'd gone. Tom shouted out.

"Matt!"

Sarah started to run towards the lake, while Tom swam over to where Matt had been. Then he dived under the water.

Sarah watched the water to see where Tom would come up again. She thought that Matt must have stepped into a deep part of the lake.

He was probably just out of his depth. To her relief, Tom's head soon bobbed up, and he was holding Matt.

Sarah waited for Tom to begin to tow Matt in to the shore, but he didn't. He seemed to be struggling to hold Matt up, and Matt wasn't helping. He was in a terrible panic. Sarah could see Tom speaking to another boy in the water, and after a moment the boy swam quickly out of the lake. Akram helped him out. By now almost the whole class was there, wondering what was wrong.

"He's stuck!" said the boy. "Matt's foot is caught in something, and he can't keep himself afloat."

Chapter 11

A Desperate Time

Akram pulled his mobile from his pocket. "We need help."

But Sarah was looking at Tom. He was holding Matt's head above the water, but Matt was still struggling.

She wondered how much longer Tom could hold Matt. She knew it wasn't safe to go to help. Matt had got caught, and she might too. There could be all sorts of hidden things, stuck in the mud at the bottom. She knew that the best way to rescue someone was not to risk your own life, but she couldn't see what else to do. The boys were too far out to rescue from the bank, Matt was trapped, and Tom couldn't hold him up much longer.

Sarah stepped into the lake.

"What are you doing?" shouted Akram. "Wait for the rescue service. They'll be here soon."

But Sarah knew that Tom and Matt might not be able to wait that long.

As soon as it was deep enough to swim, Sarah swam towards the boys. She felt much safer swimming, with her feet away from the bottom of the lake. It only took a few minutes to reach them, but at once she could see they were both in real trouble. Tom was doing his best to hold Matt but because Matt was struggling, it was getting harder and harder. Tom looked worn out.

Sarah took a deep breath and dived. The water was so churned up with mud that she could see hardly anything, but at least she was at home under water.

She soon found Matt's leg, and felt carefully for what had trapped him.

She could feel a piece of wire twisted around his ankle. The wire had pulled tight as Matt had swum up to the surface. If she was going to free his leg he would have to go right down under the water, and Sarah was sure Matt was in too much of a panic to do that.

She surfaced next to Tom. "There's some wire around his ankle," she said. "It's cutting into him, and there's no way I can get it off. You need to make sure the rescue service knows they'll need wire cutters."

Tom looked very tired but he said to Sarah, "You go back. I'll stay with Matt."

"Don't be silly," she said. "I'm fresh, but you're worn out. Go on. I can do it."

Tom took one last look at Matt and then he swam to the edge of the lake.

"Don't leave me!" screamed Matt.

"It's all right," said Sarah. "I won't leave you. But you're going to have to calm down."

Matt was hard to help. He was strong and he had been drinking. If she stayed on the surface with him he fought and struggled, and held onto her so hard that he almost strangled her. The best way was to dive, and hold him up from underneath.

In synchro she was not allowed to touch the bottom of the pool, so her training was helpful in keeping her away from the tangled wire in the mud. And she could stay underwater for ages.

But it was still tough. Although Sarah had trained hard and had good strong lungs, Abbey had never struggled against her, and the synchronised swimming routine was only a few minutes long.

At first Sarah could stay underwater holding up Matt for nearly a minute before she needed to come up to take a breath but, as she became tired, she could only hold her breath for forty seconds and then for thirty. She knew that she would have to give up soon. But would anyone else be able to help? And how could she live with herself if she let Matt drown?

Chapter 12

Exhaustion

Sarah was very near the end of her strength. Then she came up to the surface for yet another lungful of air and saw that the rescue boat was right next to her.

"Have you got wire cutters?" she shouted to the rescuers.

"Yes. Let's get you on board," they said.

"No!" screamed Matt weakly. "Please don't leave me. I'll drown!"

Sarah hung onto the side of the boat, trying to catch her breath. "Give me the cutters," she said. "I know where the wire is. Keep him afloat while I'm doing it."

Sarah took the cutters and went down one last time. She cut the wire and at once Matt's leg was free. As she headed for the surface Matt was being dragged into the boat. By accident, he kicked her head as he was pulled on the boat, and Sarah took a gulp of dirty water instead of air. Then she blacked out.

* * *

In the hospital, Sarah had lots of visitors. Tom came of course, and so did her family and Mrs Collins, as well as Abbey. And the local newspaper very soon made her into a heroine. Luckily, she had been pulled from the water very quickly, and was going to be fine. But she was kept in for a few tests before she was allowed to go home. Matt was fit to go home on the same day, and he came to see her, with his leg in a bandage.

"Thanks for saving me," he said quietly. "I'm sorry we were being so stupid with Tom."

"That's all right," said Sarah. "I'm just glad it all turned out okay."

"Will you be all right for the competition next week?" asked Abbey.

Sarah wasn't sure but she didn't want to worry Abbey. "I'll be fine," she said.

As soon as Sarah was out of hospital she and Abbey began training for the competition. They worked hard at their routine and everything seemed OK.

On the day of the competition, Abbey travelled with her parents, while Sarah and Tom went with Mrs Collins. When Sarah and Abbey came out to the pool side, Sarah could see Tom sitting with Mrs Collins. It made her feel really happy to know he was there.

The routine went well until the very end.

Sarah had to give Abbey a huge boost out of the water. Sarah had been feeling much more tired than usual and when it came to that last lift she couldn't get enough power behind it.

It wasn't a bad lift, but both she and Abbey knew that it hadn't been up to their usual standard, and they both knew that if they were not in the top three then their Olympic hopes would be dashed.

"I'm so sorry," said Sarah to Abbey as they waited for the results with Mrs Collins. "I just couldn't do the lift as well as I should have."

"You still aren't back to normal after that rescue in the lake," said Mrs Collins.

"It's not your fault."

"That's right," said Abbey. "It's not your fault."

Then the judge read out the results. Sarah and Abbey came fourth. That wouldn't be enough for a place in the Olympic team. They'd have to wait a whole four years to have another chance.

The girls couldn't help the tears that flowed down their cheeks.

On the way home, Sarah was very quiet. It was nice that Tom was there, and she knew she'd done her best, but she couldn't help thinking that she'd let everyone down.

At least people at school were more friendly. After Sarah had saved Matt's life, even Holly had stopped teasing her.

But still Sarah felt sad.

* * *

Then, a few days later, when she and Tom were on their way home from school, she got a call on her mobile from Mrs Collins.

"I've just heard from the judges," said Mrs Collins. "Are you sitting down?"

"No," said Sarah. "Why?"

"Because they've just given you and Abbey a place on the team after all!"

"What?" Sarah couldn't believe her ears.

"One of the other pairs has pulled out," said Mrs Collins. "And instead of holding another competition, the judges have decided to give the place to you and Abbey because of how well you'd done before. So you've got your chance at the Olympics!"

Sarah closed her phone.

"What is it?" said Tom, looking worried.

Sarah flung her arms around him. "We've got onto the team after all!" she told him. "We're going to be in the Olympics!"

Tom held her close. "I'm so proud of you," he whispered into her ear. And then he kissed her.